EARTHSHAKE

Poems from the Ground Up

BY Lisa Westberg Peters

PICTURES BY Cathie Felstead

Greenwillow Books
An Imprint of HarperCollins Publishers

acknowledgments

I'd like to thank Raymond Rogers of Macalester College for his review of the manuscript. Kent Kirkby, James Stout, and Richard Uthe, all of the University of Minnesota; Andy Redline of the Science Museum of Minnesota; and Peter Raimondi of the University of California, Santa Cruz, helped in answering questions. Special thanks go to my editor, Virginia Duncan, for her fresh enthusiasm and her reassuring sense of direction.

—L. W. P.

Earthshake: Poems from the Ground Up

The full-color art was prepared as collages
created from a variety of materials.
The text type is 14-point Triplex Bold.

Library of Congress Cataloging-in-Publication Data

Peters, Lisa Westberg.
Earthshake: poems from the ground up / by Lisa Westberg Peters ;
pictures by Cathie Felstead.
 p. cm.
"Greenwillow Books."
Summary: Presents twenty-two poems about geology. End notes provide
information about the earth's surface and interior, types of rocks, and how
volcanoes, glaciers, and erosion modify the landscape.
ISBN 0-06-029265-2 (trade). ISBN 0-06-029266-0 (lib. bdg.)
1. Earth—Juvenile poetry. 2. Geology—Juvenile poetry. 3. Children's poetry,
American. [1. Geology—Poetry. 2. American poetry.] I. Felstead, Cathie, ill.
II. Title. PS3566.E75573 E23 2003 811'.54—dc21 2002032177

First Edition 10 9 8 7 6 5 4 3 2 1

 GREENWILLOW BOOKS

For Dave, who drove while I wrote
—L. W. P.

To my nephews Jamie and Tom,
who are both Map Mad!
—C. F.

TABLE OF CONTENTS

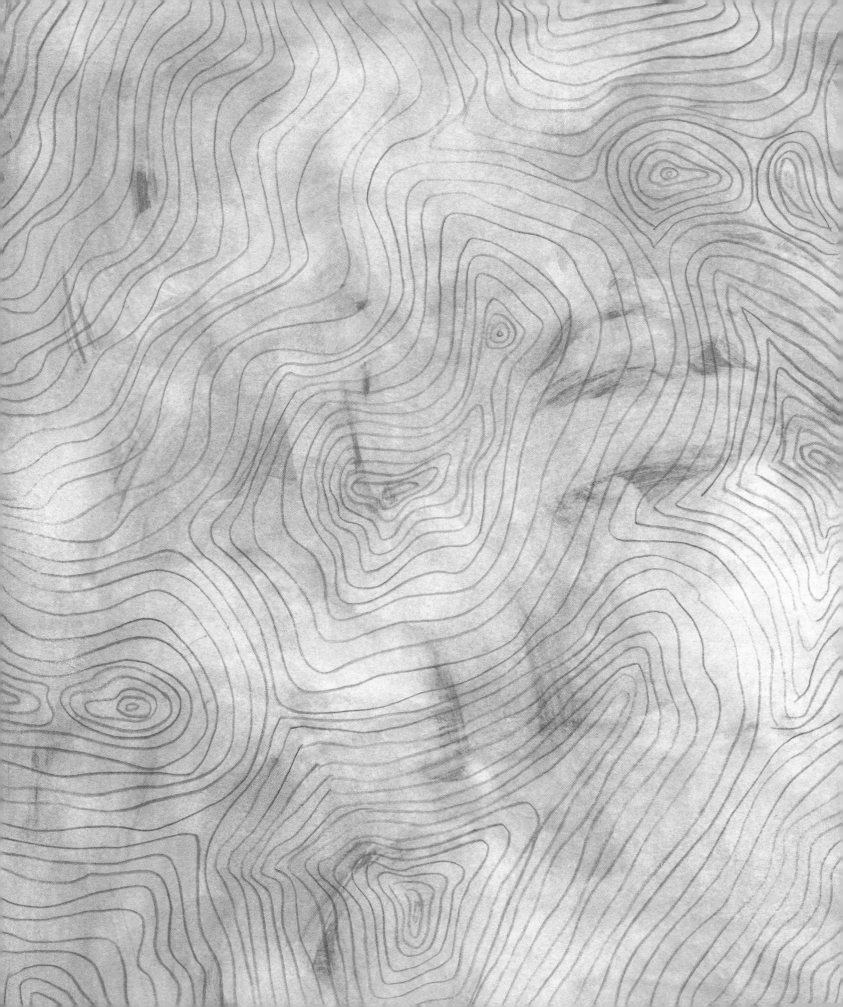

Plain Old Rock

Plain old rock
by the side of the road.

Should I roll it
into the ditch?

Round rock
by the side of the road.

I pick it up
and feel its weight.

Light rock
by the side of the road.

I take aim with my hammer
and split it.

Geode
by the side of the road.

Gleaming jewels inside.

7

Instructions for the Earth's Dishwasher

Please set the
continental plates
gently on the
continental shelves.
No jostling or scraping.

Please stack the
basins right side up.
No tilting or turning
upside-down.

Please scrape the mud
out of the mud pots.
But watch out!
They're still hot.

As for the forks
in the river,
just let them soak.

Remember,
if anything breaks,
it's your fault.

Continental Promises

Dear
Africa,
Stay close!
We'll be
friends
forever.
Love,
South America

Dear
South America,
My coastlines
are your
coastlines.
My deserts
are your
deserts.
We're rock-solid.
Love,
Africa

Wyoming Layer Cake

The earth baked a cake.

The bottom layer was black shale.
The top layer was white limestone.
And the middle layers
were a food-color assortment
of red, green, and yellow sandstone.

Take me there on my birthday.
Light candles for me
on this Wyoming layer cake
and let me make a wish:

The next time the earth
bakes a cake,
I want a four-layer marble cake
with ruby sprinkles.

Dizzy Wind

Earth,
your spinning
makes the wind dizzy.
When the wind blows
s
o
u
t
h
your spinning curls it
west
or is it
     east?
When the wind blows
h
t
r
o
n
your spinning curls it
    east
or is it
west?

Earth,
thinking about your spinning
makes me dizzy, too.

Living with Lava

Lava.
It squeezes out of a volcano
like fiery black toothpaste.
It buries a road,
a parking lot,
and a wall.

Lava.
It steams
in the tropical rain.
It hardens
in the Hawaiian heat.

Lava.
Machines with grinding wheels
crush it,
and bulldozers with wide blades
push it.

Lava.
Men and women
in work boots and hard hats
mix it with tar.
They build a road,
a parking lot,
and a wall.

Lava.
It squeezes out of a volcano.

Michigan Sahara

Sand dunes
in Michigan
are a pretend trip
to the Sahara.

When we empty
the pockets of
our jeans,
out spill
camels,
desert palms,
and scorpions.

Glacial Pace

Glacier, you are
so dull
so sluggish
so chunky.
Can't you speed it up?

Just once,
when no one is looking,
peel out!
Bulldoze a mountain today,
scrape out a valley,
scour bedrock with racing stripes.

If you get a speeding ticket,
you can
take . . . your . . . grinding . . . time . . . to . . . pay . . . up.

QuartzQuartzQuartz

We are surrounded
by quartz. It's in the
crystals of our watches, it's
in the glass of our windows, it's
in the flint of our arrowheads, it's
in purple amethysts, it's in the sand of
our beaches and our sandpaper, it's in the
granite of George Washington's chin and
Crazy Horse's nose in South Dakota, it's
in the concrete of our sidewalks
and in the white pebbles we
throw on them when we
play hopscotch.

Crumble!

Sandstone,
you have one response to life.
You crumble!
A foot falls on you.
You crumble!
The wind says hello.
You crumble!

Remember your noble past.
Your grandpa was a lagoon.
Your grandma, a dune.
You come from a long line
of deltas and sandbars.
They've passed on to you
their memories of sudden squalls
and sea monsters.
Toughen up, sandstone.

But you don't.
You crumble!

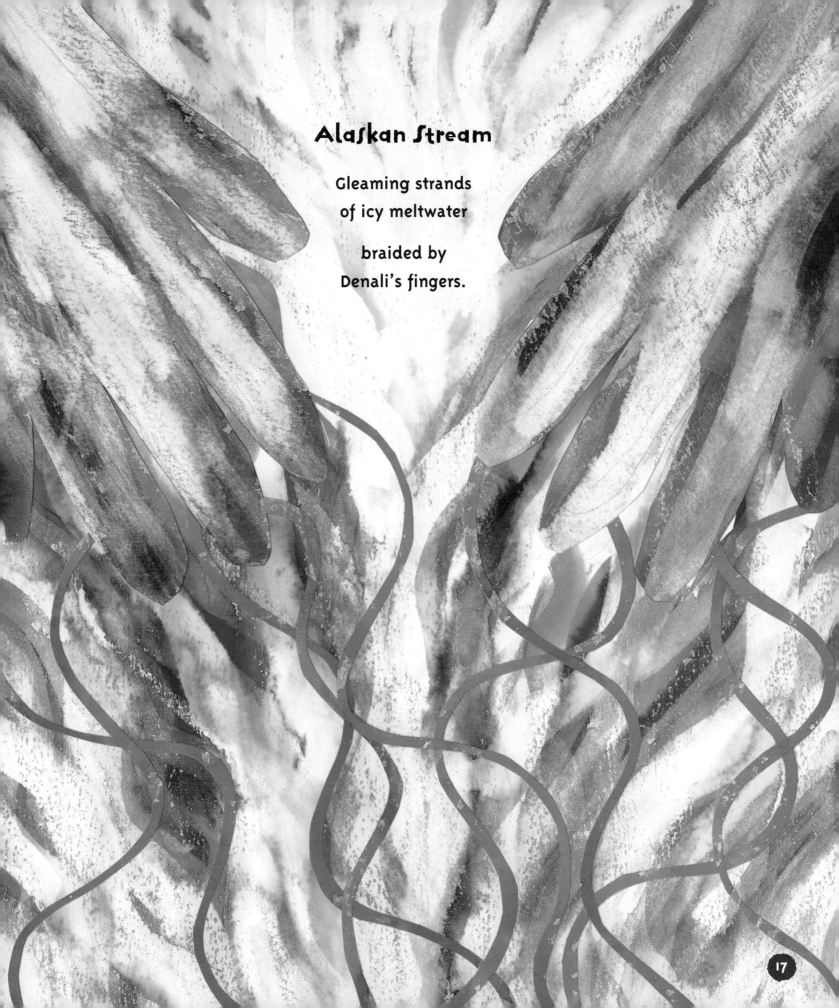

Alaskan Stream

Gleaming strands
of icy meltwater

braided by
Denali's fingers.

Earthshake

Sea cliffs
pounded into
sea caves
pounded into
sea arches
pounded into
sea stacks
by the crashing surf.

Delicious Washington coast.

River Meets Crack in the Earth

A river crosses the San Andreas fault.
It turns right, then continues on,
a little shaken up.

A Hill Named Kao-ling

A hill named Kao-ling
holds ancient, cream-colored clay
for fine china bowls.

Obituary for a Clam

Clam, Marine.
Age, 10 years.

Died 300 million years ago
in underwater landslide.
Native of the Tethys Sea.
Loving mother of 198 clams.
Lived a good life
in the shallow water
off the coast of Pangaea.
Survived by
daughter clams,
son clams,
uncle clams,
aunt clams,
clam, clams, clams . . .
She is missed dearly,
but is fossilized
in the limestone
of a backyard path
in Memphis, Tennessee.

"Earth Charged in Meteor's Fiery Death"

The earth was charged Wednesday
in connection with the fiery death
of a large meteor.

"It was a combination of gravity
and thick air," police said.
"That meteor didn't have a chance."

The meteor fell out of orbit
early Tuesday and was vaporized
as it plunged toward the earth.

"It was a fireball!"
said Jose Martinez of Sacramento.
"It lit up my whole backyard."

A hearing will be held next week.

Recipe for Granite

Melt a chunk of continent.

Heat at a million degrees,
long enough for the world
to spin a trillion times,
long enough for the Milky Way
to make it partway to infinity.

Cool
slowly enough for crystals
to form like pink and white stars,
slowly enough for the dinosaurs
to go extinct.

Makes one mountain range.
Serves a whole country.
Enjoy!

Pumice Stone Seeks Work

Lava rock
seeks employment
as bath aide.

Willing to scrape
dead skin
from elbows and heels
once a week
in exchange for
quiet, volcano-free life.

Don't Eat It

The earth:

    a spinning roll
      in the cosmic bakery

      lumpy and crumbly crust

      warm, green filling

      iron-hard jawbreaker center

Polar Confusion

What if
the North Pole
became the South Pole,
and the South Pole
became the North Pole?

Would Antarctica
lose its Ant?
Would the Arctic
gain it?

Would Santa need
a new address?
Would the penguins
trade places with
the reindeer?

Would southpaws
become northpaws?
Would the maps
be upside down

if South were North
and North were South?

The Yellowstone Whale

Deep beneath
the bubbling pools
lives a big whale.

When it breathes,
we snap pictures
of its spout.

When it flicks its tail,
the ground shakes
beneath our feet.

Stay down deep,
whale.
Stay down.

Ripples

Long ago, ocean currents
left ripples on the sandy shore.
Today, desert bedrock calls to mind
flowing water.

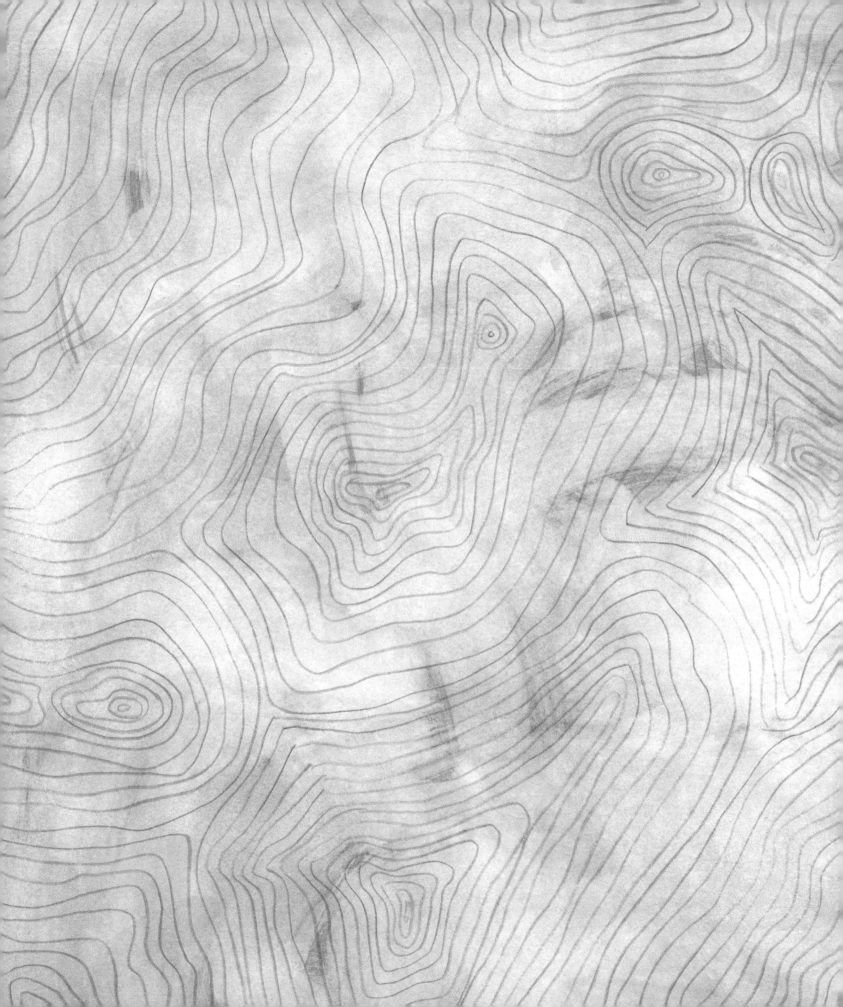

Plain Old Rock

From the outside, geodes look like plain rocks, but on the inside they are beautiful. Geodes form when groundwater rich in dissolved minerals, such as quartz, seeps into cavities in bedrock. Later, mineral crystals form along the walls of the cavities. When the bedrock wears away, the geode remains intact because it is harder than the surrounding rock.

Instructions for the Earth's Dishwasher

Some complex geological features have simple, everyday names. For example, a plate is a section of the earth's outer layer, or crust. A basin is a low area in the earth's crust. A shelf is an underwater platform at the edge of a continent. Mud pots are formed when rising steam changes rock into clay. A river is "forked" when it has more than one branch. A fault is a crack in the earth's crust.

Continental Promises

For centuries people have noticed that the west coast of Africa and the east coast of South America look as if they could fit together like pieces of a jigsaw puzzle. In the early 1900s a German scientist suggested that the separate continents we know today once formed a single large continent. He called it Pangaea.

Wyoming Layer Cake

Canyons in the American west expose layers of sedimentary rocks stacked one on top of the other. Sedimentary rock is usually made of loose particles, such as sand grains, that have been worn away and moved by wind, water, and ice. The sediments turn to rock after they are compacted, or buried and cemented together with other minerals. Each layer of sedimentary rock is formed from different materials and is laid down under different conditions.

Dizzy Wind

Because the earth spins, wind and water flowing over the earth's surface bend to the right in the northern hemisphere and to the left in the southern hemisphere. It's called the Coriolis effect.

Living with Lava

Volcanoes are formed when melted rock, or lava, is forced out of vents, or openings, in the earth's surface. Hawaii's volcanoes are made of basalt lava, which is not nearly as explosive as other kinds of lavas. It tends to ooze out, rather than explode into ash. But basalt lava is still dangerous. It can ignite forest fires and bury towns.

Michigan Sahara

Sand dunes aren't always found in deserts. For example, steep sand dunes line the south shore of Lake Superior in the Upper Peninsula of Michigan. Just behind the dunes is a forest.

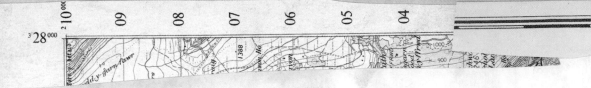

Glacial Pace

Glaciers, rivers of moving ice, creep along. But they have the power to carve out valleys and sculpt mountains over thousands of years.

QuartzQuartzQuartz

Quartz is the most common mineral on Earth. It's made of silicon and oxygen. A quartz crystal is hexagonal, or six-sided.

Crumble!

Sandstone is a sedimentary rock that feels gritty and sometimes crumbles because it is made of grains of sand. The sand grains are cemented together with other minerals, such as calcite. Sandstone can be almost any color, depending on how and where it formed. Common colors are gray, buff, and red.

Alaskan Stream

North America's highest mountain is Mt. McKinley in Alaska. The Athabaskan word for the mountain is *Denali*, which means "the high one." The streams that flow from Mt. McKinley's glaciers carry rich loads of sand and gravel. A braided stream forms when the heavy sediments are deposited as sandbars. The sandbars force the stream to divide into branching and reuniting channels, like the strands of a braid.

Earthshake

On the Washington coast, Olympic National Park features a succession of erosional forms. The relentless pounding surf finds weak spots and cracks in the cliffs. The cracks eventually widen into caves. The caves erode into arches. When the roofs of the arches fall in, the rocks that are left standing are called sea stacks.

River Meets Crack in the Earth

The earth's plates are in constant motion, like the pieces of a restless jigsaw puzzle, because of the earth's inner heat. The plate containing western California is sliding north past the North American plate along the San Andreas fault. The fault is very active, and its movement—a few centimeters per year—is marked by earthquakes. Many things, such as landforms, rivers, and roads, are disrupted by the fault.

A Hill Named Kao-ling

Kaolin (KAY-eh-lin), a fine white clay, is named after a mountain in southwestern China where, centuries ago, the clay was found and first used to make porcelain, a translucent ceramic ware. Today Chinese porcelain makers still mine the clay from the same area.

Obituary for a Clam

Clams lead relatively short lives, but if the conditions are right, their shells can be preserved as fossils in the rocks for millions of years. Clam fossils can be found in many different kinds of sedimentary rock, such as sandstone, limestone, or shale.

"Earth Charged in Meteor's Fiery Death"

Every day meteors made of stone or iron fall toward the earth from space. When they collide with the air molecules surrounding the earth, the friction from the collision heats them, and they glow. People call them shooting stars or falling stars. Most meteors burn up before they reach the earth. If they hit the earth, they are called meteorites.

Recipe for Granite

When two of the earth's plates collide, the heat and pressure of the collision melts the continental crust, and granite can form. Granite magma, or melted rock, can take more than a million years to cool. The granite core of the Sierra Nevada Mountains in California formed this way.

Pumice Stone Seeks Work

Pumice is lava shot from a volcano. It cools quickly, trapping gas bubbles throughout, and becomes a frothy volcanic glass. Pumice is light enough to float and just rough enough to scrape dead skin off elbows.

Don't Eat It

The earth has a thin outer crust and a solid inner metallic core. In between is the mantle, which is about 1800 miles deep. One of the main minerals of the mantle is olivine, an olive-green mineral. Although it is made of solid rock, the mantle is thought to flow like hot wax or putty.

Polar Confusion

The earth is a giant magnet. It has molten, or liquid, iron in its outer core. Currents in the core generate a magnetic field, or invisible lines of force between poles. Today the magnetic field starts near the South Pole, curves around in space, and converges again near the North Pole. The direction of the earth's magnetic field has reversed itself many times in the past. The sun's magnetic field reverses itself every eleven years.

The Yellowstone Whale

About four miles beneath Yellowstone National Park lies a giant pool of magma, or melted rock. The magma supplies heat for the bubbling mud pots and the steamy geysers, which are hot springs that send water into the air periodically. Yellowstone has been the scene of many volcanic eruptions and earthquakes. The last time lava flowed at Yellowstone was about 70,000 years ago.

Ripples

Sedimentary rocks, such as sandstone, can reveal the past. Scientists can see from the patterns in the rocks which way the wind was blowing in an ancient desert or which way the current was flowing along a coastline.